Sam had never seen Robert ride like this before. He never missed a beat. He never bobbled or shook. Not even his head moved. Back and forth, back and forth, up and down the driveway. It was like watching a wind-up toy. Or a robot . . .

Then Sam saw something creepy. Very creepy.

Maybe it was a trick of the moonlight. Maybe he was just too sleepy. But for a moment, Sam thought he saw the ghostly shape of a boy, standing right behind Robert on the skateboard!

Sam blinked and rubbed his eyes. When he opened them again, the ghost boy had disappeared!

To Heather Kametler

The Haunted Skateboard
Text copyright © 1996 by Susan Saunders
Illustrations copyright © 1996 by Jane Manning

Library of Congress Cataloging-in-Publication Data
Saunders, Susan.
  The haunted skateboard / by Susan Saunders ; illustrated by Jane Manning.
      p.   cm. — (The Black Cat Club ; #2)
  Summary: Four friends find an intriguing old skateboard that turns out to be haunted by the malevolent ghost of the teenage boy who was killed while riding it.
  ISBN 0-06-442036-1 (pbk.)
  [1. Skateboards—Fiction.   2. Ghosts—Fiction.]   I. Manning, Jane K., ill.
II. Title.   III. Series: Saunders, Susan.   Black Cat Club ; #2.
PZ7.S2577Hau   1996   96-19213
[Fic]—dc20   CIP
                                                                    AC

Typography by Darcy Soper
2   3   4   5   6   7   8   9   10
❖
First Edition

THE BLACK CAT CLUB #2

The haunted Skateboard

by Susan Saunders
illustrated by Jane Manning

HarperTrophy
A Division of HarperCollinsPublishers

Chapter One

"Any ghost news?" asked Sam Quirk, leaning forward on the porch steps.

The Black Cat Club was meeting at Sam's house that afternoon. All the members were there (or at least all the *living* members): Sam's across-the-street neighbor and sometimes best friend, Robert Sullivan; Sam's next-door neighbor, Belinda Marks; and Belinda's little brother, Andrew.

The four of them were drinking sodas on the front porch and not looking much like ghost hunters. But that's what they were. The whole point of the Black Cat Club was to find all the ghosts in Maplewood, wherever they might be.

"I have some news about Alice," said Belinda.

"She's not here, is she?" asked Robert.

He glanced quickly around the yard, cracking his knuckles the way he did when he was nervous.

Alice Foster was a ghost, the first ghost the Black Cat Club had found. And once they'd found her . . . they couldn't seem to get rid of her.

Alice died back in 1899, when she was only seven—exactly Andrew's age now. Maybe that's why he was the only one to have really seen her, in her long white dress and tall black shoes.

The other kids couldn't see Alice, but they usually knew when she was around. They felt an icy breeze or heard a bell jingling or smelled chocolate. Alice loved chocolate.

A visit from Alice could be really scary. After all, she *was* a ghost! And for the past week or so, she had been popping in and out of Belinda's bedroom whenever she felt like it.

"What about Alice?" Sam asked.

"I think I've come up with a way to make her leave us alone," Belinda said. "Garlic!"

"Isn't garlic for getting rid of vampires?" said Sam, who had a great memory for spells and charms and everything spooky.

"Maybe it works for ghosts, too," said Belinda. "Yesterday I lined up garlic cloves along my bedroom walls and in front of my door. And Alice didn't show up once last night."

"No wonder!" said her little brother, holding his nose. "Your bedroom stinks."

Belinda shrugged. "It's better than visits from a ghost, Andrew," she said. "And Alice makes Mittens so jumpy that he's losing weight!"

Mittens was Belinda's fat black cat. Sam thought Mittens could stand to drop a few pounds.

And he wasn't so sure that he wanted to get rid of Alice, anyway. How many clubs had a ghost as a member?

"So you really think Alice might be gone?" asked Andrew, sounding worried.

For Andrew, it was cool having a ghost around, especially one just his age who never played tricks on *him*.

"I hope so," said his sister. "You don't see her now, do you?"

Andrew shook his head. "Nope. She's not here."

He's right, thought Sam, who had another way of picking up on Alice. When Alice was nearby, there was a buzzing in his ears, a kind of secret ghost radar. And he wasn't hearing it now.

"Well, it's about time," Robert said. "We're supposed to get rid of the ghosts we find, not keep them as pets."

Alice had scared him half to death more than once.

"Let's keep our fingers crossed," Belinda said, crossing hers. "So what are we doing today?"

"We're ghost hunters, right? Let's prove that finding Alice wasn't beginners' luck. We can start at Shady Rest

Cemetery, just like last time," Sam suggested.

"I wouldn't exactly call finding Alice *lucky*," said Belinda. "And the next ghost could be even worse."

"Yeah—why don't we forget about ghosts and turn this into a different kind of club?" Robert suggested, not for the first time. "Some kind of sports club."

Robert was really good at sports. But Sam was beginning to think that *he* might be really good at ghost hunting.

"You can do whatever you want," Sam said. "I'm riding my bike over to Shady Rest."

"I'll go with you," Andrew said bravely. "Maybe we'll find Alice there."

Belinda certainly didn't want to seem like a bigger baby than her brother. She sighed, and said, "Count me in."

"Okay, okay! I'll come too," Robert said. "But we have to ride down Main Street. I want to stop by Wild Wheels and check out their skateboards."

Chapter Two

Robert had just learned to ride, on a hand-me-down skateboard from his cousin Neal. More than anything, he wanted a brand-new skateboard from Wild Wheels on Main Street.

Once they were inside the store, the other kids could see why. One whole wall was covered with totally cool skateboards, each with a different wild design painted on it.

Besides the boards, Wild Wheels sold printed T-shirts, sneakers, and caps. There were helmets, kneepads, skateboard magazines, and posters, too. Music videos were blaring from a big-screen TV.

A guy with orange hair and three gold earrings said, "Hey . . . I'm Dave. Can I help you out?"

"Not yet," said Robert. He was staring up at the skateboard wall.

Robert showed Sam and Belinda a shiny black skateboard with wavy red and yellow lines running from one end to the other. "This is the board I want," he told them.

"I like that one," Belinda said, pointing to a white board with blue and purple stars all over it.

"Girls don't ride skateboards," Robert said.

"Who says so?" said Belinda.

"Look around, Belinda. There's not a single girl in any of these pictures," said Robert.

He was right. On the posters, skateboarders were doing all kinds of stunts that didn't seem possible—like sliding down handrails backward and sailing off the tops of tall ramps. Not one of the skateboarders was a girl.

But Belinda said, "So what? There's no law against girls skateboarding."

Then she stamped out of the store. Andrew followed her. He knew better than to argue with his big sister.

"Girls," Robert muttered, already busy looking at kneepads.

Sam checked out the posters again. He'd ridden on Robert's skateboard a few times, down the sidewalk in a straight line. It was fun. But these guys were hanging in the air on their boards, some of them upside down.

It looked like they were all about to wipe out on the pavement below. Was that fun? Not nearly as much fun as hunting for ghosts, if you asked Sam.

"I'll meet you outside," he said to Robert. "And don't spend all day in here, okay? We've got places to go."

When Sam stepped out of the store, Belinda and Andrew were nowhere in sight. All four bikes were still lined up in the rack by the curb, so he knew they hadn't gone home.

"Belinda?" Sam called out.

"Back here," Belinda yelled to him. Her voice sounded sort of muffled.

Sam walked down the alley alongside Wild Wheels. At the end of it was a huge, open dumpster.

The top of the dumpster was a foot or so higher than Sam's head. A hand was waving at him from inside.

"There's tons of cool stuff in here, Sam!" Andrew yelled.

Sam climbed onto an old crate. Then he pulled himself up to sit on the edge of the dumpster.

Below him, Andrew was scrambling around among cartons full of junk, mounds of yellowing papers, and old office furniture.

Belinda stood in a corner of the dumpster, digging through the mess.

"What are you looking for?" Sam asked her from his seat on the edge.

"I'm not sure . . ." she mumbled.

Belinda shoved aside a big cardboard box and a rusty typing table.

Then she reached under a stack of newspapers and pulled hard.

Whatever she'd grabbed didn't budge.

"Help me out here, Andrew," Belinda said to her little brother.

Andrew put his arms around Belinda's waist and held on tight.

"One . . . two . . . three!" Belinda said.

They tugged. Suddenly Andrew fell backward, with Belinda on top of him.

Belinda was clutching a gray board with both hands.

"It's a skateboard," said Sam.

Belinda nodded.

It wasn't *much* of a skateboard, nothing like the ones in Wild Wheels. The board was thick and clunky and long. In fact, it looked homemade. It was painted a flat gray, and there were deep nicks in the wood. This board had been around.

Sam was beginning to have an uneasy feeling. And what was that buzzing noise?

Buzzing? It was his ghost radar! Maybe the garlic worked only in Belinda's room. Maybe Alice Foster was tailing them!

Sam peered over his shoulder. But he didn't see anything out of the ordinary. He didn't hear any bells jingling. And he didn't smell chocolate, either.

"Alice?" Sam whispered. "Is that you?"

Andrew was staring up at him.

"Are you talking to yourself?" Andrew asked him.

"Uh . . . you haven't seen Alice hanging around here, have you, Andrew?" said Sam.

"She's gone, remember?" Andrew said sadly. "Belinda got rid of her."

"I just wanted to make sure," Sam said. He stuck his fingers in his ears and jiggled them up and down. The buzzing didn't stop.

Belinda was making her way toward him through the clutter in the dumpster. "I'm going to ride this skateboard," she said.

"Well, okay. After we take a look around Shady Rest, you—" Sam began.

But Belinda acted as though she hadn't heard a word. "I'm going to ride it right now," she said. "Hold it for me, so I can get out."

Sam reached down for the skateboard. The buzzing in his ears was even louder now. Like his dad's electric razor. Or six electric razors.

It *had* to be Alice! And she had to be close.

Ghosts can change shapes, can't they? Sam said to himself.

Maybe Alice was that skinny gray cat poking around in the alley . . . or the brown bird sitting on a parking meter. Or maybe she *was* the parking meter!

While Sam was trying to spot Alice, Belinda had climbed out of the dumpster. "Sam . . . Sam, give the board back to me," she said.

Sam was handing her the skateboard when his fingers brushed across some thick scratches on the edge of it.

"Hey, look. There's something carved into the wood," he said to Belinda.

The carving was worn, and partly painted over. But Sam and Belinda could make out some letters cut into the edge of the board.

"*R . . . A . . . D*," Belinda spelled out.

"*M . . . A . . . N*," Sam finished. "Rad Man?"

Just then, Sam got an extra-loud buzz from his radar.

"Where did you find that piece of junk?" a voice called out. It was Robert, strolling down the alley. "The dumpster, am I right?"

"It's not junk! Besides, it's not the skateboard that's important. It's the skateboard*er*!" said Belinda. "And I'll prove it, here and now."

Clutching the gray board with RAD MAN carved on it, Belinda pushed past Robert. She marched toward the sidewalk. He followed right behind her.

"This is going to be good," said Robert, grinning.

Chapter Three

Andrew was still stuck in the dumpster. "Somebody get me out of here!" he yelled from inside.

When Sam pulled Andrew up onto the edge of the dumpster, he noticed that his ghost radar was quiet. But as soon as they reached the sidewalk in front of Wild Wheels, it kicked in again, like a jarful of angry bees.

Belinda was standing beside the bike rack, strapping on her bike helmet. Robert was leaning against a trash can, looking smug.

"This isn't like rollerblading, you know," he was saying to Belinda. "You don't just jump on a skateboard and start doing ollies."

"I don't even know what ollies *are*," Andrew whispered to Sam.

Neither did Sam.

Neither did Belinda. But that didn't stop her.

She set down the old gray skateboard. In a flash she was rolling along the sidewalk, her left foot on the board, her right foot pushing it faster and faster.

About a quarter of the way down the block, the sidewalk sloped downhill. Belinda planted her right foot on the skateboard too.

The board rolled forward on its own. Belinda was standing straight up on it, like a pro.

Robert, Sam, and Andrew ran down the sidewalk behind her.

"If you hurt yourself, you'll be in big trouble with Mom," Andrew warned his sister.

"Yeah, slow down, Belinda," Sam said, his ears still buzzing.

What if Alice is really mad about the garlic? he was thinking. *Maybe she's planning to play some awful joke on Belinda!*

Sam jogged up next to Belinda. "This is crazy," he said. "Wait until you get some kneepads, at least."

"I'm fine," Belinda said.

Her voice sounded a little shaky. But that could have been from going over bumps in the sidewalk.

Robert called out, "This doesn't prove anything, Belinda. Anybody can roll along on a board. *Mittens* could do it."

No sooner were the words out of Robert's mouth when something amazing happened.

The skateboard picked up speed, shooting ahead of Sam. It veered to the right . . . and suddenly Belinda and the board lifted into the air. They sailed right over a planter of petunias near the edge of the sidewalk!

"Wow!" Robert said, so surprised that he stopped dead for a moment.

Belinda made a clean landing on the far side of the planter. Then she kept on rolling.

Unbelievable, Sam said to himself. Belinda had never been on a skateboard in her life. And now she was sailing over planters!

Unbelievable—and kind of creepy.

The skateboard popped into the air *again,* and touched down on a wooden bench. Belinda and the board whizzed across the bench, glided off the far end, and dropped down onto the sidewalk.

Belinda still didn't lose her balance. She barely even bobbled.

Some older boys were walking out of a video store.

"Very hot moves for a little kid!" exclaimed one of them.

"Awesome!" said another. "Did you see that, man?" he added to a third boy.

"Really rad!" was the answer.

"Rad Man," Sam mumbled, remembering the words scratched into the gray board.

Who was Rad Man? And how had this amazing board ended up in a dumpster?

Belinda and the board were zooming toward the end of the block, where Main Street met Palmer Avenue. That was one of the busiest intersections in town!

"Belinda, stop!" Sam yelled, running faster.

"I can't!" Belinda shrieked back.

"Jump off!" shouted Robert.

But Belinda seemed to be glued to the gray skateboard. She was rolling closer and closer to the end of the sidewalk. In front of her, cars whizzed back and forth on Palmer Avenue.

"Belindaaa!" screamed her little brother. "You're gonna get kiiilled!"

Belinda began to lean farther and farther to the left. Just before she and the board were about to run out of sidewalk and fly straight into traffic, Belinda toppled off at last! The skateboard flipped over and came to a stop.

When the rest of the Black Cat Club

caught up with her, Belinda was climbing slowly to her feet.

Robert was too dazzled to speak.

Sam was sure Belinda would have plenty to say to Robert—like "I told you so!"

But Belinda seemed dazed. Her face was frozen with shock and her eyes were glassy.

Sam said, "That was incredible, Belinda! How did you do it?"

Belinda just stared straight ahead. "I d-don't know how," she stammered.

Finally Robert spoke up. "I was totally wrong about girls on boards," he said. "You're better than good. You're a natural!"

"That was so cool, Belinda," said her little brother. "Teach me how to do it!"

"No way, Andrew!" Belinda said sharply. She glared down at the skateboard as if it were her worst enemy.

"With some practice, you'll be a champion!" Robert was saying. "Hey— where are you going?"

Belinda had picked up the gray skateboard. Now she was hurrying away from them, toward Wild Wheels.

"I'm putting this thing back in the dumpster!" said Belinda without slowing down.

"I know I said it was a piece of junk. But that was before I saw what it could do!" Robert called out to her.

"Why is she acting so weird?" asked Andrew.

Belinda started running, dragging the heavy gray skateboard behind her.

The three boys followed. As they caught up to Belinda and the board, Sam's ghost radar buzzed louder. He almost couldn't believe that Robert and Andrew didn't hear it too.

"What's your problem, Belinda?" Robert said when she stopped to catch her breath. "You just made the ride of your life and you're throwing out the board?"

"There's something really . . . strange about this board," Belinda said.

"Strange how?" Sam asked her.

"When I was riding it, I didn't seem to have any control over what happened to me," said Belinda. "I tried to jump off the board before it even got to the planter. But I couldn't, somehow."

"It might be Alice playing tricks on you," Sam pointed out.

But Belinda shook her head. "No. Alice can be scary," she said, "but Alice has never tried to hurt me. When I was riding this board, I felt as though somebody else was riding it too. Somebody evil and dangerous!"

Chapter Four

"Somebody was on the skateboard with you?" Andrew squeaked. "*Who,* Belinda?"

Belinda shrugged.

But the words *somebody evil and dangerous* seemed to hang in the air over the Black Cat Club.

Then Robert spoke up. "Next you'll be telling us the skateboard is haunted! Face it, Belinda. You were so good that you scared yourself."

"There's no way I'm *that* good, Robert," said Belinda. She turned into the alley beside Wild Wheels. "If I hadn't made myself fall sideways," she added, "this board would have rolled me right into traffic. It's going back in the dumpster, before anyone gets hurt."

What if Belinda's right? Sam was thinking. *What if Alice Foster doesn't have anything to do with this?*

"Maybe we should destroy the board," he said. "We could burn it in my fireplace."

"Burn it?" Belinda shook her head. "What if there's some horrible curse on it? Awful stuff might happen to us. Let's just put it back where I found it."

But Robert hadn't given up. "I want to ask the guy in Wild Wheels if he knows anything about this skateboard," he said. "Just wait till I come back, okay?"

Robert raced up the alley toward the front door of the store.

But Belinda and Sam didn't wait. They flung the board over the top of the dumpster. Then they climbed into the dumpster themselves.

Belinda pointed toward the far corner. "It was back there, wedged in under some papers and boxes," she said.

"How did you ever see it under all of this stuff?" Sam asked, dragging the board by its wheels as he waded through the clutter.

Now his ears were buzzing like twin chain-saws. And they felt hot, as though they were overheating!

"I didn't *see* the board," Belinda told him. "It sort of . . . sort of pulled me over to it."

"Pulled you?" Andrew asked from his perch on the edge of the dumpster.

Belinda nodded. "Like a magnet. Otherwise, how would I have found it? *The board wanted out of here.*"

Suddenly Sam's arms were covered with goose bumps. The skateboard felt as heavy as lead to him.

Belinda pushed aside a cardboard box and the typing table. "Shove it back there," she said.

Sam dropped the gray board in the corner. Belinda stacked an armload of newspapers on top of it. Sam piled a couple of boxes on top of the papers. Then the two of them lifted up the rusty old typing table and added it to the mound.

Belinda wiped her hands on her jeans. "Let's get out of here," she said.

Robert was back, peering over the edge of the dumpster.

"Dave at Wild Wheels doesn't know anything about an old gray skateboard. But he said a guy named Mike might, and he'll be in the store tomorrow. So why don't we hold on to the board until we talk to him?" Robert said.

"Robert, that board is a killer!" Belinda said.

She and Sam climbed out of the dumpster.

But Robert was still arguing. "Maybe it wouldn't be dangerous for a real skateboarder," he said.

"Like *you*?" said Belinda. "Do you have a death wish? Just forget about it, Robert!"

"Okay, okay," Robert grumbled. "I'll forget about it."

But he didn't.

Chapter Five

Belinda's wild ride had worn her out. Sam's ears had stopped buzzing, but he was pretty tired himself. And Robert was in a bad mood about giving up the skateboard. Nobody felt like visiting Shady Rest Cemetery.

The Black Cat Club stopped off at Snowflake Ice Cream. They ate double-dip chocolate-fudge cones, then rode their bikes home.

Just before dinner, Sam happened to be staring out his bedroom window. That's when he saw Robert.

Robert stood outside his garage for a few seconds, looking all around. He stepped back into the garage and rolled out his bike. He glanced around again.

Certain that no one was watching him, Robert hopped on his bike. He streaked down the driveway and sped up the street.

Sam leaned out his window far enough to see Robert zoom around the corner.

It wasn't like Robert to go bike riding without asking Sam along . . . unless he was up to something. Sam hoped it wasn't what he thought it might be: Was Robert sneaking back to the dumpster?

Sam raced down the stairs to grab his own bike. But his dad stopped him before he reached the back door.

"Is your room cleaned up yet?" Mr. Quirk asked.

"Not all of it," Sam had to admit.

"Then get back up there and finish, please," his father said. "Now."

In between crawling under his bed to drag out dirty clothes and sweeping up the dustballs behind his dresser, Sam kept looking out his window. But he didn't see Robert come back home.

After dinner, Sam called him.

"Where did you go on your bike this afternoon?" he asked Robert.

"This afternoon? Oh, you mean *this* afternoon," Robert stalled. "I went to the store for my mom," he said. "She needed some . . . butter."

Sam hoped it was the truth. But he doubted it.

Before he went to bed, Sam crept down to the kitchen. He eyed the garlic bulbs in a wire basket on the counter. But he grabbed a handful of his mom's fancy chocolate candies instead and hurried back upstairs. He knew Alice would love the chocolate. And just in case she decided to visit *him,* he'd rather she be happy than angry!

That night, Sam dreamed about skateboarding. He was riding the gray skateboard with RAD MAN on the side, rolling faster and faster down the steepest hill in Maplewood.

At the bottom of the hill, a car was stalled in the middle of the intersection.

Sam was going to have to jump right over it!

But the skateboard started to wobble. The faster it rolled, the more it rocked. And the more Sam shook!

"If we crash, I'll be creamed!" Sam yelled in the dream as he shook and shook.

Suddenly Sam woke up, in his bedroom in the dark. But he was shaking in real life . . . *because his bed was bouncing up and down!*

"Yooow!" Sam yelped, grabbing on to his headboard.

Then he heard a little bell ringing somewhere in the darkness. That is, he heard it as well as he could around the buzzing in his ears.

"A-Alice?" Sam whispered. "I b-brought you some chocolates."

Although maybe garlic would have been a better idea after all, he thought.

The silvery tinkling of a bell was his reply. And his bed stopped bouncing up and down.

Sam scooted up until his back was pressed against the headboard. He wondered what to do next. He'd feel better if it weren't quite so black in his room. . . .

Sam reached out slo-o-owly to turn on the lamp next to his bed. But before his hand touched the switch, he heard the lamp sliding away from him.

Sam jerked his arm back and pulled the covers tight around his shoulders.

He swallowed hard. "Wh-what do you want?" he whispered.

Tomorrow—if there *was* a tomorrow—he'd buy a ton of garlic!

Suddenly his curtains sprang open. Moonlight shone through the window and lit up the room.

Sam didn't see anything like a girl in a long white dress. But the silvery bell rang faster and faster.

Then the bedroom window flew up with a screech. A second later, Sam's covers were snatched out of his hands!

Bzzzzzzzz, his ghost radar hummed.

Sam wanted to plug up his ears, squeeze his eyes shut, and stay that way until the sun rose. But somehow he couldn't. He watched his covers float all the way across the bedroom and halfway out the open window.

Sam still didn't move. Now Alice's bell rang again, even louder, and that icy breeze ruffled Sam's hair.

All of a sudden, Sam's legs slid sideways. But he hadn't moved them! Then his feet hit the floor. And—one heavy step at a time—he found himself walking toward the open window.

What was Alice doing? Maybe she wanted to push *him* out the window like the sheets!

Sam braced himself and waited for a shove from behind. He was hoping that he'd land in the soft bushes outside the living room. . . .

But nothing happened. The bell stopped ringing. He smelled chocolate, as if Alice were offering him a treat. And Sam felt calmer—calm

enough to look out the window.

That's when he saw Robert. Again.

Across the street, Robert glided up his driveway in the misty moonlight. He was riding a skateboard, as silently as a ghost.

Chapter Six

Now Sam realized what Alice wanted. She wanted to show him Robert.

Robert rolled down the driveway to the street, flipped the board around in midair, and glided back toward the garage. Robert and the board sailed over the back steps and touched down near the closed garage door. Then they made a half circle up and across the door.

Sam had never seen Robert ride like this before. He never missed a beat. He never bobbled or shook. Not even his head moved. Back and forth, back and forth, up and down the driveway. It was like watching a wind-up toy. Or a robot.

What color was the skateboard that Robert was riding? Was it the light blue one from Neal? Or was it gray, like the one in the dumpster?

Sam couldn't tell, not in the moonlight.

The buzzing of his ghost radar had stopped. Alice was gone.

Sam sat down in a chair by the window. He rested his arms on the windowsill. His eyelids were getting heavier and heavier. He yawned and put his chin on his arms.

The tenth or twelfth or twentieth time Robert rolled down the driveway, Sam saw something creepy. Very creepy.

Maybe it was a trick of the moonlight. Maybe he was just too sleepy. But for a moment, Sam thought he saw the ghostly shape of a boy, standing right behind Robert on the skateboard!

Sam blinked and rubbed his eyes. When he opened them again, the ghost boy had disappeared, and Robert was rolling farther down the driveway.

Sam tried to keep watching. But

soon he fell into a dreamless sleep.

"Sam! Sssst! Sam!" A loud whisper awakened him.

Sam opened his eyes. It was just starting to get light outside. And Belinda was standing in his yard, staring up at him.

For a split second Sam didn't know how he got where he was: slumped on the chair, his head on the sill of his open window. His sheet and blanket were hanging down the side of the house.

Then he remembered his visit from Alice.

He looked over to his dresser. The chocolate candies that he'd left there were gone.

And he remembered Robert's midnight ride!

Sam scrambled to his feet, half expecting to see Robert still gliding up and down on a skateboard. But he wasn't. The Sullivans' driveway was empty.

"Why were you sleeping in the window?" Belinda asked from below him.

"Shhhh . . . I'll tell you in a minute. Stay there," Sam answered in a low voice.

He pulled on some clothes and his sneakers, and tiptoed downstairs. Belinda was waiting for him at the door.

"What are you doing up so early?" he asked Belinda.

"Mittens didn't come home last night," she said. "Sometimes he gets locked in the Sullivans' garage by mistake, so I'm on my way over there."

"I'd like to check out the Sullivans' garage myself," Sam said.

He told her about Alice's visit and about Robert's midnight ride. "Alice wanted me to see Robert on the skateboard," he ended. "I'm sure that's why she came to my room last night."

"Do you think it was *his* skateboard he was riding?" Belinda asked. "Or was it the gray one?"

"I couldn't tell," Sam said. "But

Robert has never ridden so well. It was like he was programmed."

"But when could he have gone back to the dumpster?" Belinda asked.

"I saw him leaving the house on his bike just before dinnertime," Sam answered. "Later, he told me he was doing an errand for his mom. But it sounded like he was making it up."

"If Robert has the gray skateboard . . . he's in big trouble!" Belinda said. "Let's get over there and see what we can find."

Chapter Seven

The neighborhood was quiet. No one on Mill Lane seemed to be awake except Sam and Belinda. They dashed across the street and up the Sullivans' driveway.

The garage door was closed. The side door to the garage was locked.

"Bummer!" Sam muttered.

"We'll climb through a window," Belinda told him. "I've done it before, to rescue Mittens."

They crept around to the back of the garage. Belinda pushed the window up just far enough for them to crawl through it.

The garage was crammed with lots

of stuff besides the Sullivans' two cars. The walls were lined with gardening tools, fishing poles, and lawn chairs. A big water heater stood in one corner.

"Mittens? Mittens," Belinda called softly.

A sleepy *meow!* was her answer.

"I knew it! He loves the seat covers in Mrs. Sullivan's car," Belinda said.

She slipped past a lawn mower to get to the green car. Sam started looking around the rest of the garage.

The light blue skateboard, the one that had belonged to Robert's cousin, was hanging on the back wall. But Sam kept poking around, behind a wheelbarrow and under a beach umbrella. Then he edged around the cars, heading toward the far corner of the garage and the water heater.

Before Sam was halfway there, his ears started buzzing.

Sam said, "Over here, Belinda." He needed some company.

Belinda was carrying Mittens. The

black cat was half asleep in her arms. But as Belinda walked closer to the water heater, Mittens started to growl deep in his throat. His yellow eyes widened. The hair on his back stood straight up.

Then, with a hiss and a yowl, Mittens leaped out of Belinda's arms. He dashed across the garage and sprang through the open window.

"There's something weird going on," Belinda said to Sam.

The two of them squeezed past Mr. Sullivan's black car and into the corner. Sam peered around one side of the water heater, Belinda the other.

"I see a piece of gray wood," Belinda said.

"Pull it out," said Sam.

"*You* pull it out," Belinda said, backing away.

Sam reached behind the water heater.

The heater was warm. But when Sam's hand touched something icy cold, he knew they'd found it: *Rad Man's gray skateboard.*

Sam dragged it out and let it drop onto the garage floor. He and Belinda stared at it uneasily.

It didn't look spooky or dangerous: a clunky, beat-up old skateboard, covered with nicks and scratches. But Sam thought about the boy ghost that he *might* have seen riding it. . . . And his ears buzzed like a dentist's drill.

Sam and Belinda glanced at each other.

"Now what?" Sam said.

"We get rid of it," Belinda said. "Again. Before it's too late!"

"What do you mean, 'too late'?" said Sam.

"I think it can take over your life, if you let it," Belinda said grimly.

Sam remembered Robert riding back and forth, back and forth: Was he a kid whose life could be taken over by a skateboard?

It sure looked that way.

Chapter Eight

Sam and Belinda lifted up the skateboard by its wheels. They carried it across the Sullivans' garage and pushed it through the back window. Then they crawled out themselves.

"Let's get this thing as far away from Robert as we can, before he wakes up," Sam said.

"We could take it to the recycling center," Belinda said.

The recycling center was several miles from Mill Lane, on the far side of Maplewood. Once they'd dumped the gray skateboard in one of the huge garbage bins, Robert would never find it.

Sam nodded. "Let's do it," he said.

The sun was higher now, and the residents of Mill Lane were beginning to stir. Sam and Belinda had to wait until Mr. Minihan, two houses down, walked to the end of his driveway for his morning paper and back.

Then they raced across the street into Sam's yard, holding the gray board between them. They slipped into the Quirks' garage, out of sight.

"I'll get my bike," Belinda said.

To Sam, alone in his garage with the spooky skateboard and buzzing ears, it seemed like an hour before Belinda came back. But it was more like five minutes.

She wasn't by herself, though. Her little brother was with her.

"Hi!" Andrew whispered loudly.

"Why did you bring him?" Sam muttered to Belinda.

"It was faster than arguing," Belinda said. "He'll have to keep up as best he can."

She helped Sam strap the skateboard

to the frame of his bike.

Then they were off, streaking down Sam's driveway and up Mill Lane.

"Main Street to Lambert Road?" Belinda asked as they sped around the corner.

"It's fastest," said Sam.

Most of the shops on Main Street were still closed. But Andrew said, "The lights are on in Wild Wheels."

As they rolled closer, they saw a man sitting on the front steps, drinking a cup of coffee.

Didn't Dave at Wild Wheels say something about a guy named Mike? Sam turned his bike in at the curb. "Are you Mike?" he asked.

"That's me," said Mike. He had lots of curly hair and a droopy mustache. "What can I do for you?"

Sam pointed to the gray skateboard strapped to his bike. "Dave thought you might know something about this board," he said.

"Homemade job," Mike said, looking

it over. "And it's old. Boards just aren't this big anymore."

"There are some words carved into the edge," Belinda told him. " 'Rad Man.' "

"Rad Man?" Mike grinned. "Now, there's a name I haven't heard in years," he said.

"You know Rad Man?" Sam said excitedly. They were finally getting somewhere!

"*Knew* him," said Mike. "Long hair, always wore a black T-shirt with a red skull and roses. And when it came to skating, he was totally out of control."

" 'Knew him'?" Belinda repeated. "Where is he now?"

"He took one chance too many," said Mike. "I don't remember what happened, exactly. But when he was around fourteen, he wiped out big-time. Permanently. . . . He's dead," Mike added, in case they hadn't understood. "Been dead and gone for at least twenty years."

A chill ran down Sam's spine.

"Dead," Belinda murmured. "But maybe not *gone*."

The buzzing in Sam's ears sounded like a jackhammer.

"Well, we'd better get moving," Belinda said hurriedly.

"Thanks," Sam said to Mike.

"No problem," said Mike.

Sam climbed carefully onto his bike, trying not to touch the skateboard strapped between his knees.

As they rolled down Main Street, Belinda said, "Rad Man will be out of our lives in ten minutes. Fifteen minutes, tops."

But the farther they got from Wild Wheels, the harder it became for Sam to pedal. By the time he turned onto Lambert Road, it felt as though his bike tires were rolling through sticky tar. Or as though he were dragging a great weight along with him, like a dead elephant, or . . . a dead Rad Man.

Belinda was whizzing along. She wanted to get to the recycling center as fast as she could. Andrew was pedaling hard to keep up with his sister. Neither of them noticed that Sam had fallen behind.

Finally, Sam shouted, "Hey, Belinda!"

She squeezed on her brakes and skidded to a stop at the top of a small hill. Andrew pulled up beside her. They both looked back toward Sam, puzzled. Then they rolled down the hill until they reached him.

Sam was standing next to his bike, puffing and panting. "What are you waiting for?" Belinda asked.

"There's something weird going on," Sam said. "I'm having a hard time pedaling."

"I'll take the board for a while," Belinda said.

Sam started to unstrap the skateboard, but Belinda said, "No, don't touch it any more than you have to. We'll trade bikes."

"Sure," said Sam. Whatever put some distance between him and the gray skateboard was fine.

The three of them started up the hill again. But by the time they'd reached the top, Belinda was huffing and puffing like Sam had been.

"I don't understand this—I can ride ten miles without getting out of breath!" Belinda said. "Unless . . ." She looked down at the gray skateboard.

"It's the board," Sam said. "It doesn't want to leave us."

Chapter Nine

"We'll *push* the bike to the recycling center if we have to!" Belinda said.

A few blocks later, that's exactly what Sam, Belinda, and Andrew did. They had to force Sam's bike forward along the side of the road, the gray skateboard still strapped to the frame.

Andrew held on to the left handlebar of Sam's bike, while he rolled his own bike along with his left hand.

Belinda held on to the right handlebar. She was rolling her bike along with her right hand.

Sam walked behind Belinda, pushing with all of his strength against the back of his bike seat. But the bike barely moved.

"We'll be lucky if we get to the center by next week," Belinda said.

"Or ever," mumbled Sam.

"Belinda, I'm hot. I want to go home," Andrew whined.

"Forget it," said his sister. "We're all in this together."

But Andrew let go of Sam's handlebar.

"It's too heavy for me," he said. "I'm just a little kid."

Andrew sat down right where he was.

Sam was dead tired himself. "I don't think we're going to make it to the center. Not this way, Belinda," he said.

"Then how?" Belinda said, glaring at the gray skateboard. "We have to get rid of this thing."

Suddenly the air around them began to swirl. It whipped into a tiny whirlwind.

The whirlwind drew up dirt and sticks and paper and dead leaves from the side of the road. It spun the litter

around Sam and Belinda, and tried to push them around, too.

"Hang on to the bike, Belinda!" Sam yelled.

They squeezed their eyes shut as dirt pelted their faces. Sam heard Belinda's bike crash to the ground. But he didn't let go of his own bike, with the board strapped to it.

The whirlwind twirled away from them, ruffling bushes and trees as it went.

"Where did that come from?" Belinda said, picking a stick out of her hair.

Andrew was on his feet, practically hopping with excitement. "It was Alice!" he said. "Didn't you see her? She started spinning around and around, really fast. And she made the wind happen!"

Sam's radar was humming, but so faintly he could barely hear it.

"That's just great! If Alice doesn't want us to get to the recycling center, we're sunk," Sam said gloomily.

"The Black Cat Club will be stuck

with this evil skateboard for the rest of our lives," Belinda added.

Then Andrew said, "There was a boy here too."

"What boy?" Sam said.

"A boy with long hair. He ran away when Alice made the wind happen," Andrew said.

"I thought I saw someone on the skateboard with Robert last night," Sam told Belinda. "Sort of a boy . . . ghost."

They stared at each other.

"Rad Man had long hair," Belinda whispered.

All at once, Sam's bike began to roll forward. . . .

"Help me out here!" Sam said, still hanging on to the seat.

Belinda scrambled to her feet and grabbed a handlebar. "Get on, Sam!" she said.

Sam jumped on his bike. The minute his feet touched the pedals, he was off in a cloud of dust!

Before, it had seemed as though

something—or someone—was holding him back.

Now it felt like something—or someone—was pushing him forward. Sam's ears were buzzing louder and louder.

"Thanks, Alice," he murmured.

He had never biked so fast in his life. Sam raced up Lambert Road, bounced over the railroad tracks, tore around the curve, and turned left onto Fulton Avenue. Belinda and Andrew could barely keep up.

Sam sped across the bridge over the Windsor River, and turned right onto Dover Lane, which took him—and the skateboard—straight to the Maplewood Recycling Center!

Chapter Ten

Sam waited for Belinda and Andrew just inside the gate of the recycling center. The three of them rode their bikes up the ramp beside the four huge garbage bins.

Belinda helped Sam unstrap the gray skateboard. Together they tossed it over the railing, into the last of the containers.

"Out of a dumpster, back to a dumpster," Belinda said, sort of like a magic charm.

Then a man in a Fanelli's Seafood truck tossed a couple of big trash cans full of smelly clamshells on top of the skateboard.

"That's that," said Belinda.

"Rad Man is history," said Sam.

Sam, Belinda, and Andrew rode back toward Mill Lane feeling free and easy.

"Want to come for breakfast, Sam?" Belinda asked. "Dad makes waffles on Saturdays."

"I'd better get home," said Sam.

The three of them turned onto their street. The first thing they saw was Robert, riding toward them on his bike.

"Hi!" Andrew called out.

"Where are you going?" Sam asked Robert as they rolled nearer.

Robert didn't seem to see them. He glided right past them, and they could hear him mumbling to himself: *"Ollie frontside grab. Backside lip-slide. Kick-flip . . ."*

Then Robert turned left onto State Street.

"I think that was skateboard talk," said Sam.

"Weird!" said Andrew.

"He's mad because he knows we took his board," Belinda said.

"He'll get over it," said Sam.

After dinner that evening, Sam was poking around in his garage, trying to find his bicycle pump, when he heard Belinda yell his name. She sounded really upset.

"I'm in here!" he yelled back, stepping out of the garage.

Belinda was standing at the end of Sam's driveway, pointing across the street.

"Look!" she said.

It was Robert, gliding down his own driveway on Rad Man's board!

"How did he find it?" Sam murmured.

"It just pulled him—all the way to the recycling center!" said Belinda.

As Sam and Belinda watched, Robert flipped the board around in midair at the end of his driveway. He rolled back toward his garage, sailed over the steps, touched down near the closed garage door . . . made a half circle up

and across the door. And started down the driveway again.

That's when a bell started jingling.

"Do you hear that?" Sam said. His ears were buzzing, too.

"Yeah. It's Alice's bell. . . ." Belinda barely breathed the words.

"I don't have a good feeling about this," Sam said, moving closer to the street.

Robert had reached the end of his driveway again. But instead of flipping the board around, he kept right on going, out onto Mill Lane.

Chapter Eleven

"Belinda, jump on with him!" said Sam.

If they both jumped on the skateboard with Robert, maybe they could weight it down enough to make it stop!

Sam didn't allow himself to think for more than a second about Rad Man, who could be standing on the board too. He raced down his driveway to the street, ran up alongside Robert, and hopped onto the skateboard.

Sam grabbed Robert's shirt to steady himself. "Hey, it's me!" Sam said.

But Robert didn't seem to realize that Sam was standing right behind him.

"Inside hard flip-grabbed indy to fakie," he muttered. *"Ollie frontside grab."*

A few seconds later, Sam felt Belinda hop on the board.

"Made it," she murmured, holding on to Sam's waist. Then she yelled, "Andrew, no!"

But her little brother had raced out of the house and caught up with them. He landed on the end of the board with a thud. Now all four members of the Black Cat Club were squeezed together on a skateboard, rolling down Mill Lane.

Sam figured the board would grind to a halt in a minute or two. Four kids on a board was over two hundred pounds of weight. Mill Lane was pretty flat, and no one was pushing the skateboard forward with his foot.

So why were they going faster and faster?

They veered left around the corner, onto State Street.

"I don't like this . . ." said Belinda.

"Maybe we should jump off," said Andrew. Then he shrieked, "I can't jump off! I can't move my feet!"

Sam couldn't move his feet either. They were stuck to a skateboard that was completely out of control!

Faster, faster . . . the mailboxes and parked cars they passed were a blur.

In fact, everything around them looked hazy, as if they were rolling through a cloud. Sam began to feel sort of peaceful—until he spotted a ghost on the front of the board!

It was Rad Man.

Rad Man was balanced right on the tip of the skateboard, riding backward to face them. He was bigger and older than they were—around fourteen, Mike had said.

Rad Man had long, messy hair. He was wearing a black T-shirt with a red skull and roses on it, and cutoffs. And he was grinning.

It wasn't a friendly grin. Rad Man really wanted to scare them to death. Or just kill them, whichever came first!

"Belinda, do you see . . . ?" Sam murmured over his shoulder.

"I see him, all right," Belinda whispered. "Where is he taking us?"

Sam shook his head.

Where was Alice Foster when they really needed her?

Chapter Twelve

They were zooming along so quickly, it was impossible for Sam to tell exactly how far they'd gone. After the runaway board had streaked down State Street, it turned only once, a right onto Lambert Road.

Robert still hadn't spoken, except to mumble, *"Backside smith-grind."*

The kids were squeezed so tightly together that Sam could hear Andrew whisper, "Maybe he's taking us back to the recycling center, Belinda."

Why would Rad Man be doing that? Sam asked himself.

But he couldn't come up with anything that made more sense—until he heard the whistle of the eastbound express train in the distance.

Suddenly Sam knew, without any doubt, what Rad Man had in mind. He was going to smash the four members of the Black Cat Club under the wheels of the eastbound express as it thundered through town.

This ghost wants company! thought Sam. Then there would be *six* ghosts to haunt the kids of Maplewood, if you counted Alice.

Sam heard Belinda whisper, "The train's coming."

He twisted his body from side to side, trying to break loose from the killer skateboard.

"Sam, you'll knock us all off!" Andrew yelled from behind him.

"I don't think we'll be that lucky!" Sam yelled back.

He wouldn't mind crashing to the concrete. At least that would mean they weren't racing to their doom!

Rad Man was having a great time. His

shoulders shook as he laughed at them silently.

Now Sam could hear the train engine rumbling down the tracks, and the click of its wheels speeding toward the crossing on Lambert Road.

"The gates'll be down. He won't be able to get close to the train," Andrew shouted. "Will he?"

A narrow piece of wood at a train crossing wouldn't stop Rad Man! *Nothing would stop him.* He had died on a skateboard, and he wanted them to die on one too.

The train was rushing closer and closer to Lambert Road. The skateboard was zooming closer and closer to the crossing. Rad Man laughed and laughed.

"Stop!" Belinda shrieked at the ghost. "This isn't fair!"

All at once there was a *whoooosh*!

A great gust of wind shook the board and everyone on it. Then the wind swirled around them in a circle, slowing them down.

It must be Alice!

Rad Man looked surprised. Then he looked frightened.

And Robert made sense for the first time that day. "Wh-Where am I?" he stammered. "What's happening?"

The wind blew harder and harder. It spun them first one way and then another, until Sam couldn't tell if they were headed *toward* the train or *away* from it.

But he could still hear the express roaring closer and closer.

Suddenly the wind sucked them right off the board! It tumbled them down beside the red-and-white train-crossing gate on Lambert Road.

The express train thundered past them at about a hundred miles an hour!

Sam rubbed dirt out of his eyes and blinked a few times. He saw a little girl in a long white dress and tall black shoes standing on the pavement. Smiling, she bent down to give the gray skateboard a shove. It rolled right

under the wheels of the eastbound express.

In seconds, the haunted skateboard was wood chips!

There was an eerie howl. The ghost of Rad Man was clinging to the side of the train as it clattered out of sight.

For the moment, Alice was gone as well—except for a strong smell of chocolate.

"I saw her!" Sam yelled. "I finally saw Alice Foster!"

"So did I," said Belinda.

"I did too," said Robert.

Andrew said, "I've seen Alice Foster a hundred times." He sniffed the chocolate in the air. "I'm hungry," he added. "And it's getting dark. How will we get home?"

"How did we get *here*?" asked Robert.

"It's a long story," said Sam. "Do you remember last night, in your driveway?"

Robert shook his head.

"Then it's a *really* long story," said Belinda. "How about if we tell you everything over chocolate sodas at Snowflake Ice Cream? We can call my mom from there."

"We'll get an extra chocolate soda, just in case Alice shows up!" said Sam.